Rain Forest Adventure

Written by Gare Thompson

Illustrated by Tom Barrett

STECK-VAUGHN®
COMPANY
ELEMENTARY • SECONDARY • ADULT • LIBRARY

dam had gone to the zoo with his parents and his little sister, Jess. Their favorite part was the rain forest area. It had many interesting animals.

"I loved the snakes," said Jess.

"The monkeys were the best," said Adam.

"Well, now we know how it feels to be in a real rain forest," said Mom as she wiped her face.

Dad said, "What a long day! We sure spent a lot of time looking at the animals." Jess nodded and hugged her toy snake. Her eyes closed as she fell asleep in the car.

Adam said, "I think I'll name my monkey Jake." Mom and Dad smiled. It had been a great day.

4

When they got home, Dad said, "Off to bed, Adam. And you too, Jake."

Adam put Jake on his dresser and got into bed. "I'm glad I got you. You're my rain forest friend," Adam said to Jake. Then Adam yawned and fell fast asleep.

Soon Adam began to dream that he was in a rain forest. Tall trees with huge leaves were growing everywhere. They formed a roof over him. Adam couldn't even see the sun.

The rain forest felt hot and sticky. Adam could see mist rising from the ground. He could hear birds singing above. Then he saw a narrow path. Adam began walking down the path.

The path led Adam deep into the rain forest. It was almost dark. The tree branches looked like fingers that were long and curled.

Adam heard a hissing sound over his head. He looked up. It was a snake, wrapped around a branch!

Adam ran down the path before the snake could move. Then he heard a roar behind him. Was it a jaguar?

Adam looked around. The snake was gone, and there was no jaguar behind him. Suddenly, the leaves above him moved. Adam jumped right off the path. He looked up to see Jake!

Jake said, "Don't be afraid, I'm here to help you."

Adam said, "I think I'm lost. Can you help me find my way out of here?" Jake took Adam's hand and started to lead him out of the rain forest.

Adam followed closely behind Jake.
They tiptoed right past a sleeping jaguar.
They walked below some singing birds.
Then they sneaked under a huge snake
wrapped around a branch.

Suddenly, it started to rain. The path became muddy and slippery. Adam and Jake could barely see where they were going. Then there was a loud crash. Adam jumped!

Adam woke up with a start. He wasn't in the rain forest. He was in his own bed! He looked out his window. It was raining hard outside. A tree branch was crashing against the house.

Adam sat up and saw that Jake was no longer on the dresser. He felt something in his bed. He looked down. There was Jake, right beside him!